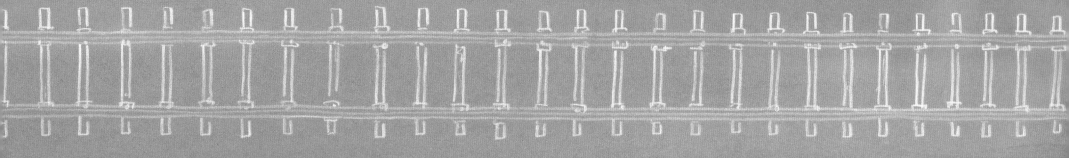

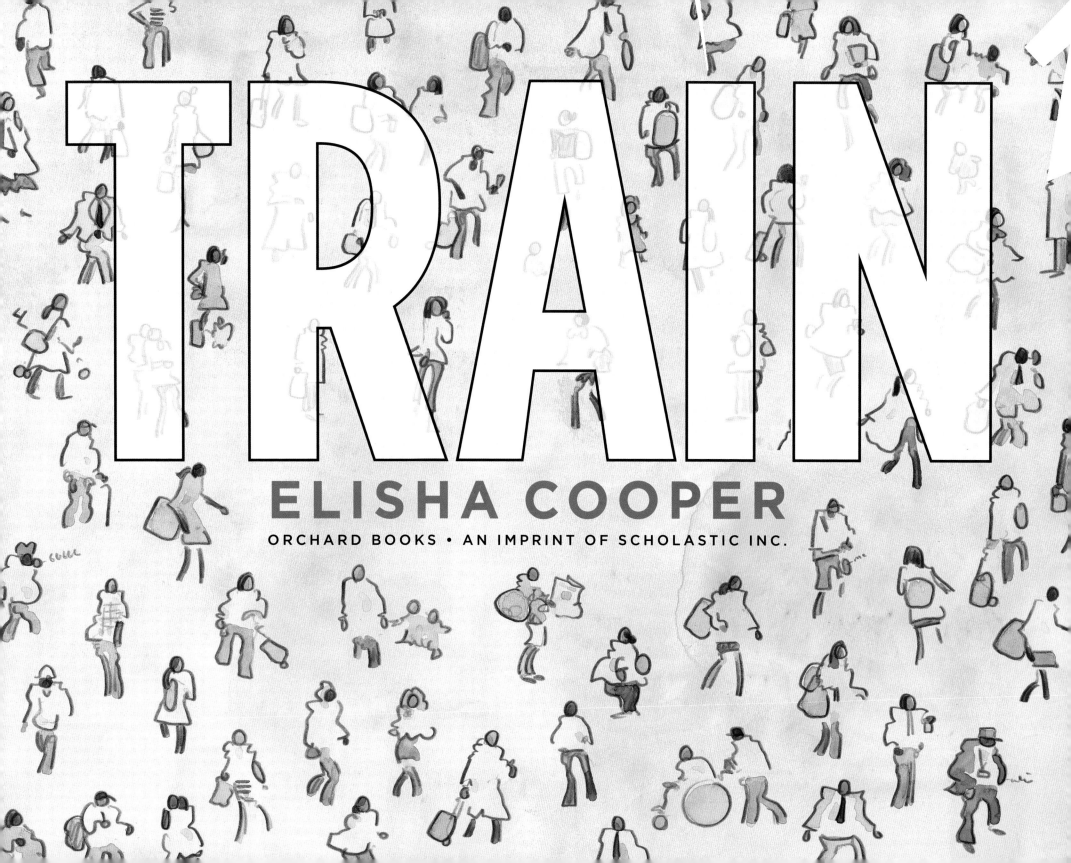

TRAIN

ELISHA COOPER

ORCHARD BOOKS • AN IMPRINT OF SCHOLASTIC INC.

The train leaves in minutes. Passengers buy tickets and rush across the floor to where the train is humming on its tracks. Conductors look up the platform. They check their watches.

One minute. Hats wave, whistles blow. *"All aboard!"* Not all.
A passenger jumps on at the last second. The doors whoosh shut.
The train pulls out of the station . . .

. . . and out of the city. The train is a red-striped Commuter Train. The conductor swings down the aisle, shouts, *"Tickets please!"* and snaps holes in the tickets with his punch.

The train clatters past ball fields and bridges, past backyards and ponds. Main streets flash by. The view changes every second. Hello town, good-bye town. On to the . . .

. . . next town. The Commuter Train slows with creaking brakes. Announcements crackle. Some words get lost: *"We are arriving at Ghblighrrfzze."* The train stops at a small station. Passengers off, passengers on.

As the Commuter Train waits, another train roars past on another track. A larger train. A bright blue Passenger Train hurrying between cities. The train is late so . . .

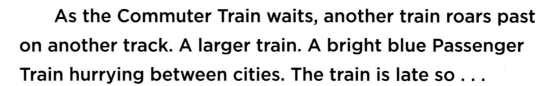

. . . up in the cab of the engine, the engineer pulls back the throttle. The Passenger Train powers forward. It hurtles past barns and farmhouses. The engine is so big it makes other big things look small.

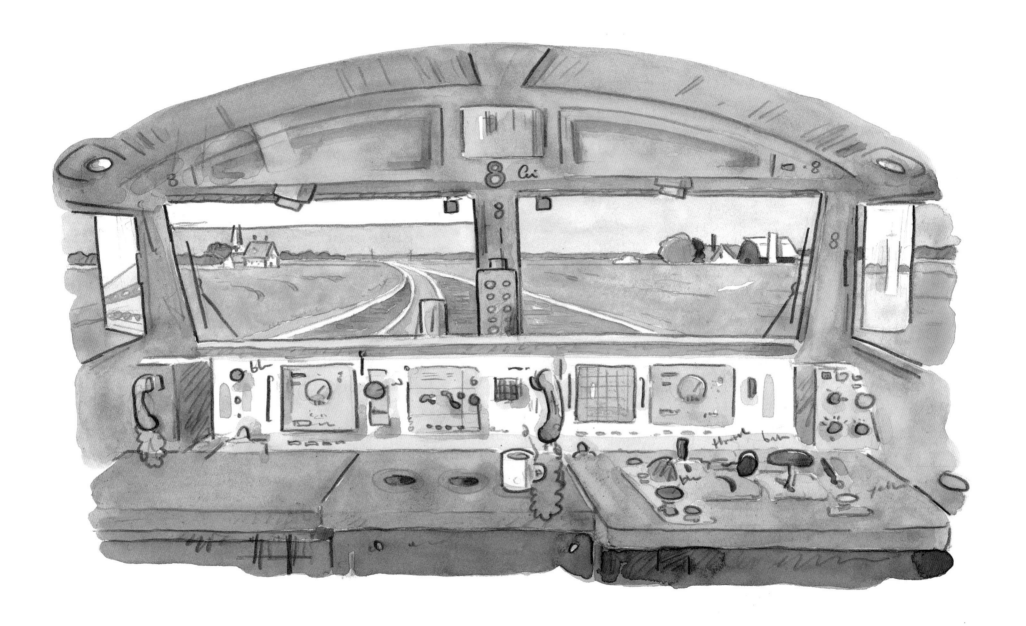

The engineer sits very still but his fingers are always moving. Pushing levers, turning dials. He taps a blue button— *long, long, short, long*—and the horn blares out . . .

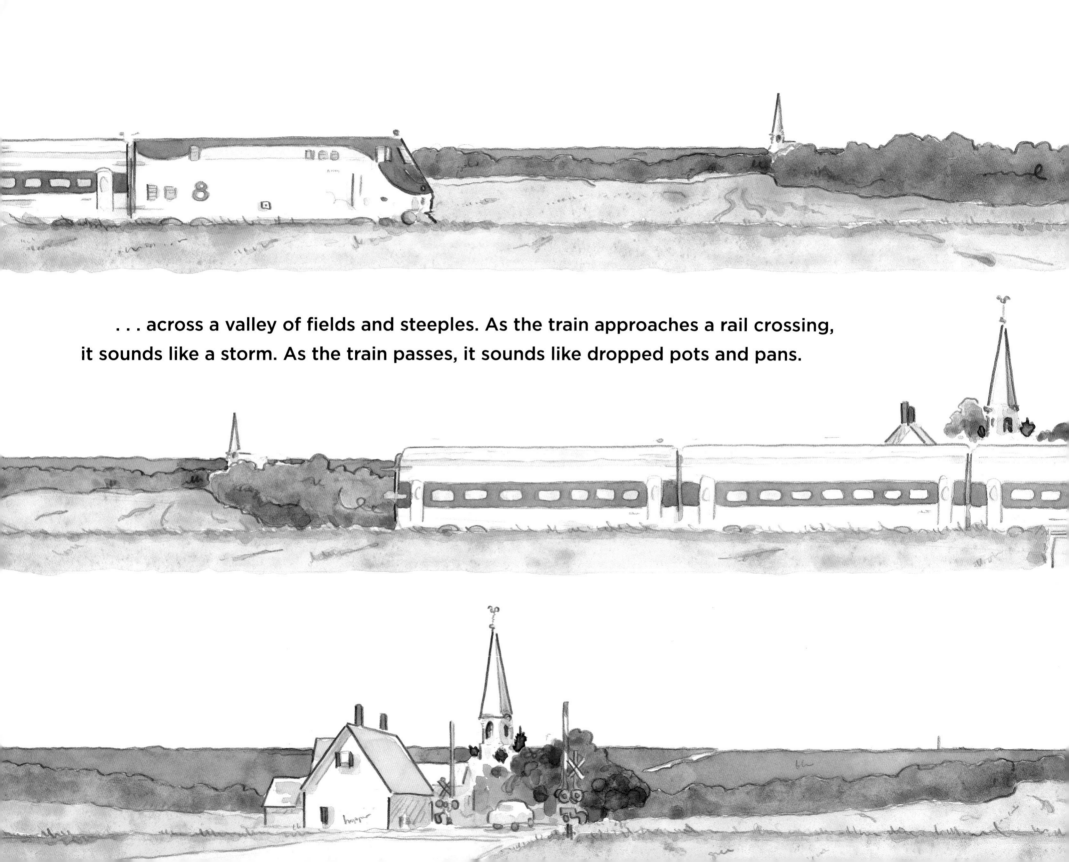

. . . across a valley of fields and steeples. As the train approaches a rail crossing, it sounds like a storm. As the train passes, it sounds like dropped pots and pans.

As the train leaves, it sounds like the *da dum da dum* of a beating heart.
Then, silence. But up ahead the Passenger Train keeps going, thundering into . . .

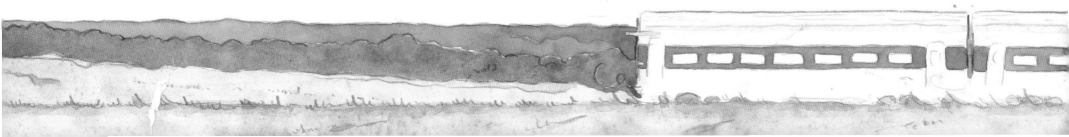

. . . the outskirts of a midwestern city filled with smokestacks and factories and belching steam. Tracks weave in and out. Small animals scurry under the tracks.

The Passenger Train crawls over the tracks through a jungle of gravel, wires, and dirt. Everything smells of grease and rust and burnt toast. The train lurches . . .

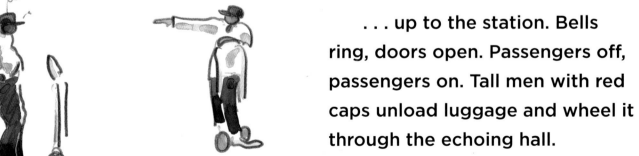

. . . up to the station. Bells ring, doors open. Passengers off, passengers on. Tall men with red caps unload luggage and wheel it through the echoing hall.

In the rail yard next to the station, another train works. An orange Freight Train loading up. It grumbles under its breath as railcars are hauled and hitched to its back. The railcars are filled with . . .

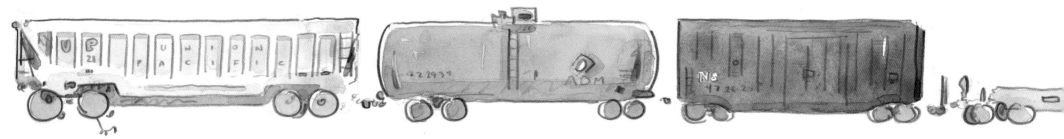

. . . steel, concrete, oil, wheat, corn, and lumber. Things used to make other things. Sturdy things. All crammed in containers the color of tomatoes and eggs.

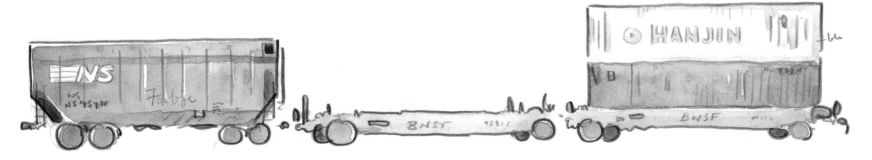

Thick white letters cover the railcar sides. Graffiti paints their sides, too. After the railcars are linked into one long train, the Freight Train creeps out of the city and . . .

. . . across the Great Plains. It rolls past wheat and prairie grasses. Past silos and barbed wire. Past a lone hawk circling under a big western sky. The Freight Train rolls slower than slow.

So slow it's hard to tell it's moving. As if the train and the clouds above were having a race to see which can go slower. Slow, *sloooow.* And like the clouds, the train does not stop . . .

. . . even as it inches up among low hills. Then, another train passes.
A dark green Overnight Train switchbacking westward. It climbs over
the Rocky Mountains through snow flurries and pine forests.

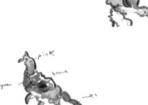

The train curves along icy rivers and shoots through tunnels *(where its chatter turns into a whisper).* There are no roads outside. Just eagles, elk, and turkeys. As the sun lowers, passengers gather in . . .

. . . the dining car, where the waiter sways down the aisle with her tray. She doesn't spill a thing. Plates of meat loaf, potatoes, ice cream, and pie. A movable feast.

In the sleeping car, two girls unfold seats into beds and make the room their own. Little sink, little shower. Everything little. The girls sleep as the train curls through the mountains and . . .

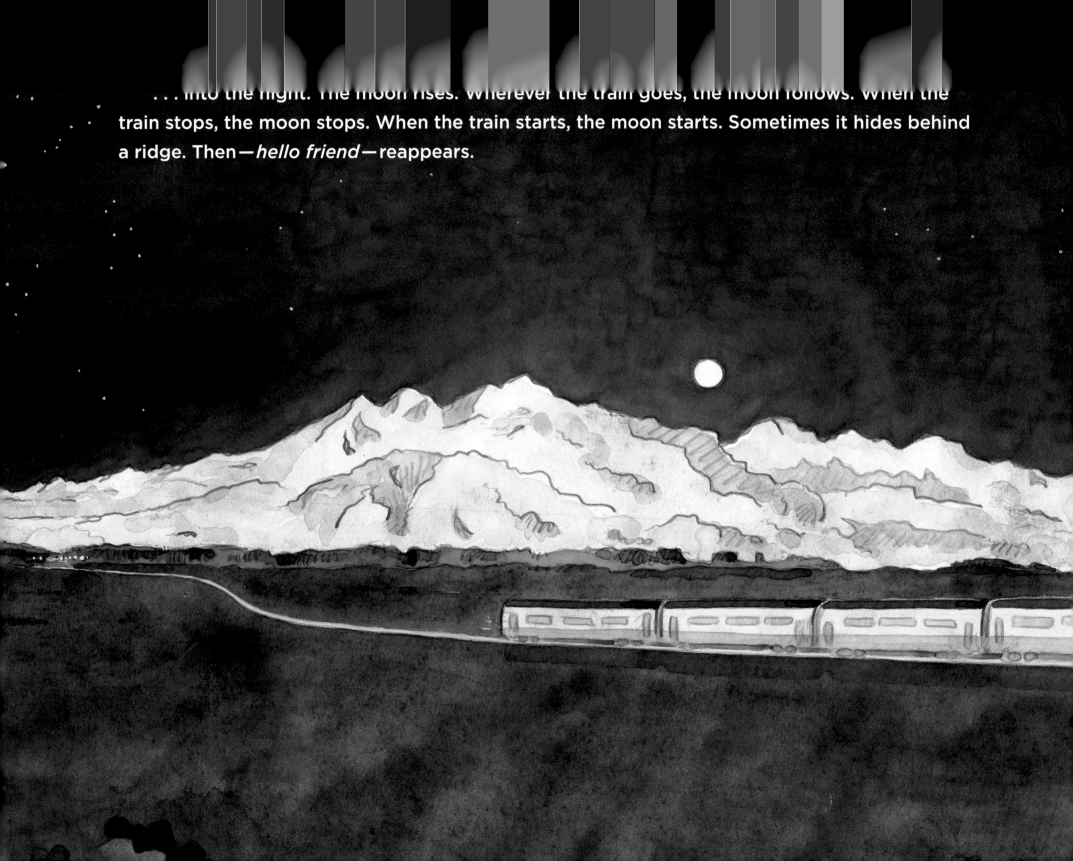

. . . into the night. The moon rises. Wherever the train goes, the moon follows. When the train stops, the moon stops. When the train starts, the moon starts. Sometimes it hides behind a ridge. Then—*hello friend*—reappears.

The train rests in small towns. Passengers off, passengers on. Stars blink in the cold air, lights blink on the horizon, and the Overnight Train pushes into the deep hours of the night . . .

. . . and wakes to morning sun. Passengers wake to biscuits, butter, jam, and coffee. Outside, everything is different. Mountains have turned into orchards, snow into grass, boulders into cattle.

Now, accelerating into view across a wide green valley, one last train passes.
A sleek and white High-Speed Train, blurring a streak across the land. *Schwooosshhh . . .*

. . . *shhhh.* The High-Speed Train flies. It glides over bridges and marshes, by bays and highways. Inside, it is cool and quiet. The train is a small world moving through a larger world.

Passengers read or type. One whispers in her phone: *"We're almost there. We'll see you soon."*
The High-Speed Train races toward the city on the coast and the passengers prepare for . . .

. . . the end of their journey. They close their books, they pack their bags, they think about what's next. A clean bed, a warm dinner. They are almost home.

And with a slowing turn into the station and an easing of speed and a sigh of brakes and a gentle last *thunk*, the train stops.

GLOSSARY & NOTES

Brake The brake is the lever the engineer pushes to make the train slow down.

Conductor The conductor is in charge of the train. Responsibilities include following the schedule, making announcements, and taking tickets.

Container Containers are big metal rectangular boxes filled with cargo and stacked on flatbed cars.

Dining car The dining car is a restaurant on wheels with a kitchen that serves breakfast, lunch, and dinner.

Engine The engine powers the train. Some engines are electric (their power comes from wires along the track), and some are diesel (their power comes from fuel inside the engine).

Engineer The engineer drives the engine and sits in a cab at the engine's front.

Freight Train A freight train carries cargo, not people. Some have a hundred cars and are powered by up to four engines. A single freight train can be over two miles long.

Horn The horn sounds when the train approaches a rail crossing. It was once operated by a cord; now it's a button.

Punch The punch is a handheld tool that makes holes in tickets. Each conductor's punch is different: ◖ ★ ! ♥

Red Caps Red Caps are workers who carry passenger luggage. Their tradition of wearing red hats started so they would stand out in a crowd.

Schedule The schedule lists the time that trains arrive and depart. In New York's Grand Central Terminal, trains leave one minute after their scheduled departure time. So the 8:08 leaves at 8:09.

Sleeping car The sleeping car is a moving hotel, with small individual compartments whose seats fold out into beds.

Switchback A switchback is a zigzagging track that allows a train to ascend or descend a steep slope.

Throttle The throttle is the lever the engineer pulls to make the train speed up.

For the Great Plains

Copyright © 2013 by Elisha Cooper

All rights reserved. Published by Orchard Books, an imprint of Scholastic Inc., *Publishers since 1920*. ORCHARD BOOKS and design are registered trademarks of Watts Publishing Group, Ltd., used under license. SCHOLASTIC and associated logos are trademarks and/or registered trademarks of Scholastic Inc.

No part of this publication may be reproduced, stored in a retrieval system, or transmitted in any form or by any means, electronic, mechanical, photocopying, recording, or otherwise, without written permission of the publisher. For information regarding permission, write to Orchard Books, Scholastic Inc., Permissions Department, 557 Broadway, New York, NY 10012.

Library of Congress Cataloging-in-Publication Data Available

ISBN 978-0-545-38495-7

11 10 9 8 7   21 22 23 24 25

First edition, October 2013
Printed in China   38

The text type was set in Gotham Medium. The display type was set in Gotham Bold Condensed. The art was created with watercolor and pencil.
Book design by David Saylor and Charles Kreloff

AUTHOR'S NOTE

I rode a lot of trains for this book. Many details are taken from real life (like the clock in Grand Central Terminal). Readers may notice that I combined details (the interior of Philadelphia's 30th Street Station with the exterior of Denver's Union Station) and made some up (the San Francisco station is purely imaginary). So this book is accurate, to a point. My thanks to all the train people who helped me.

Scholastic Inc., 557 Broadway, New York, NY 10012.

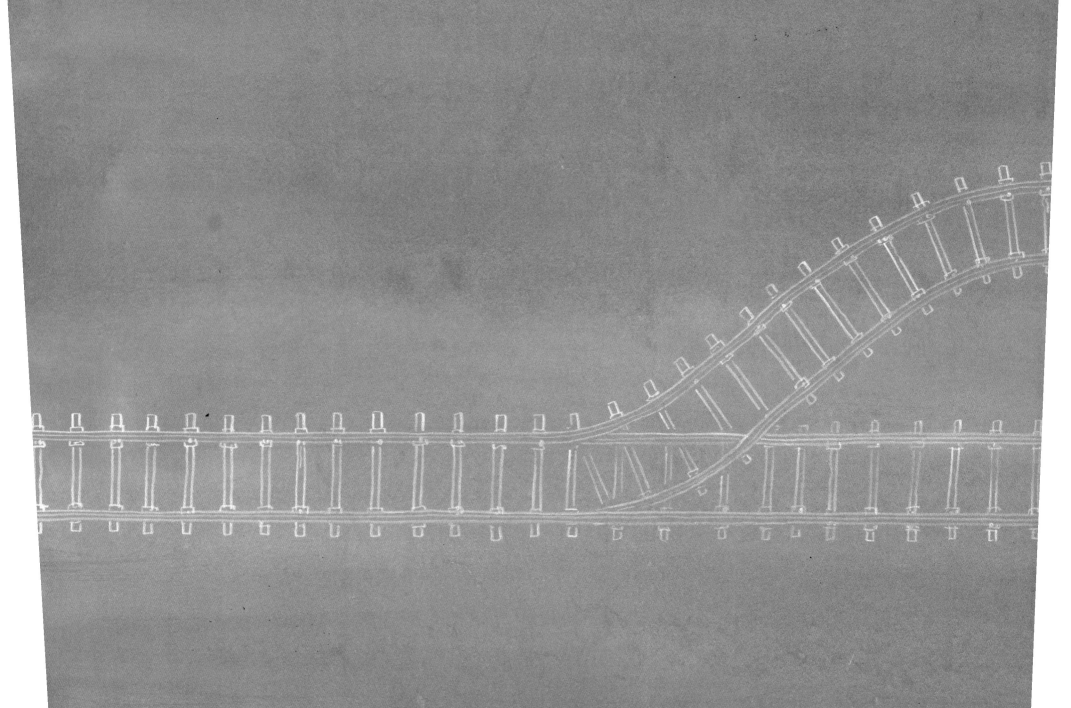